A YEAR
WITH MOLLY
AND EMMET

MARYLIN HAFNER

FRIENDS
FOR EVER!

CANDLEWICK PRESS
CAMBRIDGE, MASSACHUSETTS

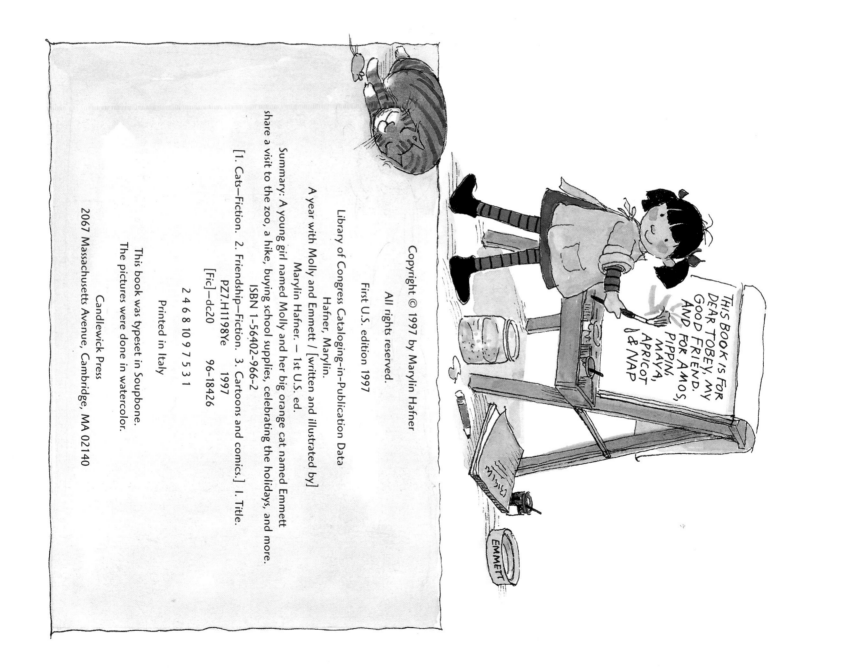

First U.S. edition 1997

Library of Congress Cataloging-in-Publication Data
Hafner, Marylin.
A year with Molly and Emmett / [written and illustrated by]
Marylin Hafner. — 1st U.S. ed.
Summary: A young girl named Molly and her big orange cat named Emmett
share a visit to the zoo, a hike, buying school supplies, celebrating the holidays, and more.
ISBN 1-56402-966-2
[1. Cats—Fiction. 2. Friendship—Fiction. 3. Cartoons and comics.] I. Title.
PZ7.H1198Ye   1997
[Fic]—dc20   96-18426

2 4 6 8 10 9 7 5 3 1

Printed in Italy

This book was typeset in Soupbone.
The pictures were done in watercolor.

Candlewick Press
2067 Massachusetts Avenue, Cambridge, MA 02140

INTRODUCTION

WHEN MY MOM IS WORKING AT HER DRAWING BOARD, SHE LETS ME DRAW AND PAINT NEARBY. I HAVE MY OWN CRAYONS AND PENCILS, AND I TRY TO BE QUIET.

ONE SNOWY DAY I WAS JUST SCRIBBLING ON A BIG PIECE OF PAPER, AND SUDDENLY, A FLUFFY ORANGE CAT APPEARED. "HELLO," HE SAID, "MY NAME IS EMMETT." EMMETT NEVER TOLD ME WHERE HE CAME FROM AND I FORGOT TO ASK.

WE HAD FUN. MOM MADE BROWNIES AND EMMETT HELPED CLEAN UP AFTERWARD.

HE CAME TO LIVE IN OUR HOUSE AND WE'VE BEEN FRIENDS EVER SINCE.

THIS BOOK IS ABOUT OUR TIMES TOGETHER IN SPRING, SUMMER, FALL, AND WINTER. WE HOPE YOU ENJOY IT.

LOVE, MOLLY AND EMMETT

SPRING

SUMMER

FALL

WINTER